A Special Gift

G. Clifton Wisler

Baker Book House
Grand Rapids, Michigan 49506

Copyright 1983 by
Baker Book House Company

ISBN: 0-8010-9661-8

Printed in the United States of America

1

Waking up on a winter morning was never easy, but for Pip to stir himself from the comfort of his warm bed on that last school day before the Christmas holidays was next to impossible.

"Pip, get up!" his mother shouted down the hall. "Come on, Pip, you're too old for me to have to wake you up!"

"All right," he moaned, rubbing his bare feet together as a defense against the cold.

The winter had been cold for Texas. There had already been two days of snow, and the house never really got warm. His mother was trying to keep the heating bill down, so Pip learned to sleep in the cold by using three blankets.

"Are you up, Pip?" his mother asked again.

"Sure," he sighed, sitting up in the bed.

Pip yawned deeply, then slid out of the blankets onto the floor. He grabbed his robe and wrapped it around him. He wore only a tee shirt and pajama bottoms to bed, and the cold bite of the air penetrated to his skin.

Pip shook away the cold and trotted down the hall to the bathroom.

"About time you got up," his mother said to him, flashing the special smile that always crossed her face whenever Pip was around. "You'd better hurry if you want breakfast."

"You said the magic words," Pip said, laughing. "I'll get myself ready and be there in a flash."

"You'd better, kid," she said. "I might just eat everything myself."

"Not you, Mom," Pip told her with a smile. "You're on a diet, remember?"

"You little terror," she yelled, chasing him into the bathroom.

Mornings around the house were always like that. Since all Pip had was his mother, and all she had was Pip, they laughed and joked and played around a lot. But he didn't have any extra time that morning to play around. He ran in and out of a warm shower, then hurried to dry off.

"Breakfast is almost ready, Pip," his mother told him through the bathroom door. "Hurry up!"

"I have to get my hair dry and dress. You wouldn't want me naked and dripping wet, would you?"

"Don't be funny, young man," she said "Get with it!"

Pip reached over and took the blow dryer in his small hand. He switched it on, feeling the hot air warm his neck and tickle the backs of his ears. As his blond hair fluffed into place, he brushed a few uncooperative hairs back over his forehead.

There were still three strands hanging in his left eye,

the same three strands which never seemed to stay where they belonged. Pip told himself that if he couldn't get them to stay where they belonged, he'd get his mother's scissors and cut them off.

He brushed the unruly strands back into the thick locks that hung over his forehead. Satisfied, he wrapped the robe tight around him, grabbed his discarded sleeping clothes and raced across the hall to the bedroom.

Pip could smell his breakfast cooking, so he hurried to dress. He put on his clean white slacks, then slid on a pair of bright green socks and polished black slip-on shoes. Then he slipped a tee shirt over his bony shoulders, managing to upset his carefully brushed hair.

"Great!" he yelled, slamming his hand down on the bed.

"Are you coming to breakfast, Pip?" his mother called.

"Just a second."

Pip reached into his closet and took out a white shirt. He had only two white shirts, and he hated to wear them. He had to today, though, because the school choir was performing, and the boys and girls had orders to dress in white. Pip buttoned his shirt, stuffed his shirttail under his belt and raced into the kitchen.

"Pip, your hair is all messed up," his mother said. "I wanted you to be just perfect for today."

"I will be," he said, taking the plate of food she handed him. "I just have to brush it again."

"You'd better put on a sweater first. That green one you got from your grandmother would be nice."

"I planned on it," Pip said through a mouthful of pancakes.

"Don't talk with your mouth full."

Pip chewed and swallowed before saying anything else.

"Mom, I even have my green socks on. Look," he said, raising his left leg in the air to show her his sock.

"I didn't need a demonstration," she said. "Now eat."

Pip turned his attention to his breakfast. The pancakes soon disappeared. When he was nearly finished, his mother looked at him seriously.

"Pip, how do you feel about Christmas this year?" she asked.

"Fine. Christmas is Christmas."

"How would you like a little change this year?"

"Are we going somewhere? Is Dad coming to see me?"

"No," she said, frowning. "Pip, do you still miss him?"

"I don't know," he said, matching his mother's frown. "He's my father. I guess if he doesn't miss me, I don't miss him."

"Hey," she said, lifting his fallen chin. "Don't let it worry you. He never paid much attention to me, either. We don't need him."

"It'd be a lot easier on you if he were around."

"Well, now that you mention it, I have an idea. What would you say to a Christmas visitor?"

"Who?" Pip asked, suspecting something was up.

"A friend of mine, His name is Tom Paxton. He's from New England originally. He's been in Boston for a year, but he's coming back to town tonight."

"You know him pretty well, huh?" Pip asked.

"Yes, Pip. We were very close in college. Since then I've worked with him on several projects."

"He's in advertising then?" Pip asked.

"Not exactly. He's called a commercial artist."

"He draws commercials?" Pip asked, laughing.

"No, silly," she said, laughing back at him. "He designs things. He draws ads. He's also quite a cartoonist."

"Do you want him here?"

"Yes, Pip. I haven't asked a man to share this house since your father left. I thought for a while he'd come back. It's been seven long years now, and I think it's time we both had another man around."

"I don't want another father," Pip said. "I didn't have much luck with the first one."

"Pip, you'll like him. I just know it."

"Mom, this is just like when you kept taking me over to Mr. Barnett's house every Saturday. And the whole business about me playing baseball last summer. And going to Y camp."

"Okay, Pip. Look, I know you hate to admit it, but you enjoyed baseball. You didn't mind that week at camp, and even old Mr. Barnett was better than another Saturday of twenty-year-old movie reruns."

"I don't need anyone, Mom," he protested.

"Neither one of us believes that, Pip. But I didn't invite Tom here for you. I invited him because I like him, and I'd like to share our Christmas with him."

"But it's *our* Christmas, Mom. It's *our* time to share. I don't want an outsider here."

"Look, Pip, he's down here all alone. His family is up in Vermont. You and I know what it's like to feel

7

lonely. Now do you want me to call Tom and tell him you want him to stay by himself?"

"I guess not," Pip said with a big frown.

"Hey," she said, lifting his chin a second time. "It won't be death. You'll have someone to keep you company when I'm shopping. He'll entertain you. You can play the piano for him."

"Big deal," he grumbled.

"I'd like you to be a little more excited about this, Pip. No matter what's in your mind right now, Tom is a very good man. Most men run for the nearest exit when they hear I have a twelve-year-old son. Tom told me he thought it was great. He likes kids. He's from a big family, and . . ."

"I'm not his son!"

"I didn't mean to say you were. But I'd like you two to be friends."

"Where's he going to sleep?" Pip asked.

"Well, I think it'd be a nice gesture for you to offer your room to him."

"More bad news."

"What do you say?"

"It's all right," he said, frowning. "Could you turn up the heat, though. The living room is freezing at night."

"Deal," she said.

"When's he coming?"

"Tonight."

"Tonight?" Pip said, standing up. "You know our choir program's tonight. Mom, you promised to come. You missed all the others. You promised to come!"

"Promises get kept around here," she said. "I'll pick

up Tom and we'll both be there. I talked to Mrs. Marshall, and she'll take you when she takes John. Okay?"

"Just fine," he said, looking at the floor.

"Now I have a favor to ask of you. Will you promise to be on your best behavior while Tom's here? No worms in his shoes or ants in his bed? No turning off the water in the middle of a shower?"

"I only did that at camp," Pip said.

"What about the ice cubes you put in your Aunt Anne's bedclothes last Christmas?"

"I'll be good," he said.

"Promise?"

"I promise," Pip said, standing up. "Now I'd better get my sweater on and straighten my hair."

"Put on a necktie, dear. I want you to look your best."

"Nobody wears a tie, Mom," he protested. "Not even John Stephens does that, and he's so straight he could hide behind a telephone pole."

"You'll wear one today. Now go get into your sweater and let me have a crack at your hair. I want to take a picture to send to Mother."

"Doomed," Pip said, trudging to his room to get the tie.

He found a green tie and slipped it around his collar. Then he wiggled into his sweater and walked to the bathroom.

"I thought you'd tie the necktie, Pip," his mother said.

"I can't," he told her. "You know I never can tie the knot."

"Well, maybe Tom can teach you."

"Do commercial artists wear ties?"

"To church," she said, laughing. "I think you'll have a chance to find out all about commercial artists."

She raised his collar and put her warm arms around his neck. It felt good to lean against her as she tied the knot in his tie. When she finished, she fixed his collar and turned him around to pass inspection.

"Not a very good knot, huh?" she asked.

"It'll pass," he said.

"Now let's fix your hair."

She took the brush and smoothed out the upset hairs. Then she patted him on the shoulder and gave him a big kiss.

"What's the kiss for?" Pip asked.

"It's Christmas."

"Some answer," he said, smiling at her.

"Pip, remember your promise. A promise is always to be kept, right?"

"Always. I've never broken a promise in my whole life, Mom. And no matter how awful he is, I'll keep this one."

"He won't be awful, Pip."

"Well, if he makes you happy, he can't be all bad."

"Oh, you!" she said, putting her arm around his frail shoulder.

"I love you, too," he said, giving her a hug.

"What am I going to do with you when you get big? You've already figured me out. You read me like a book. If I get mad, you just smile your way out of trouble."

"That's called natural charm," Pip said. "Grandma says I have it."

"Well, I know one thing you don't have. Modesty. You're sure not afraid to brag about yourself."

"Well, nobody's perfect," Pip said, laughing.

"How would you feel about a ride to school?" his mother said, walking to the closet to get their coats.

"It sure beats a five-mile walk. Let's go."

2

Pip jumped out of the car in front of the school, waved good-bye to his mother and raced off to the gym where the junior high kids who arrived early gathered.

Pip wove his way through the other young people to where his friend, John Mulligan, was waiting for him.

"Hey, John," Pip said, sliding across the bench beside his friend. "You ready for Santa Claus?"

"Knock it off, Pip," John said. "Is that a tie you've got on?"

"Sure is," Pip said, swallowing hard. "Gives me a distinguished look, don't you think?"

"You look strange, Pip," John told him. "The other guys are going to think you hit your head on the door or something."

"Don't you think a guy should get dressed up for something as important as a choir concert? I mean if a guy won't get dressed up for a concert, what will he get dressed up for?"

"Don't start that with me, Pip. I've been around you too many Saturday afternoons. You can con your mom and my mom and every woman in the neighborhood, but you can't tell me it was your idea to wear that tie. A green tie? You look like a Christmas tree."

While John laughed, Pip turned a bright shade of red.

"I tell you, some friend you turn out to be. I expect to have you backing up everything I say, and you laugh at me," Pip said, a huge frown covering his face.

"Well, I'm sorry, Pip. But remember, I didn't wear a green tie to school."

"Your mom could bring you one."

"Forget it, Pip. I wouldn't wear a green tie if Beth Ann Lawrence asked me to."

"If you did, Beth Ann might notice you."

"If I did, everybody would notice me," John said, laughing loudly.

They didn't talk anymore about the tie. Pip joked his way through most of the kidding heaped on by the other kids, but the compliments he got from some girls and teachers was more than he could stand. After second period, the tie went into his locker for the rest of the day.

At lunch Pip and John sat together at their usual place in the cafeteria. The cafeteria staff were serving their version of country-fried steak. It was a cross between a chicken-fried steak and an old tennis shoe. It looked like the first and tasted like the second.

Pip usually ate anything since he cooked his own dinner half the time. That was no treat. T.V. dinners were only one step above the school cafeteria. But today he had no appetite at all.

"You still brooding over that green tie?" John asked him.

"No, it's something else. Something Mom told me this morning."

"She finally told you the truth about Santa Claus, huh?"

"Funny," Pip said, giving his friend a fake smile.

"Is it about your dad? Did a letter come or something?"

"No chance of that. Once Dad got his new wife, that was that. I haven't even had a post card in four years. The last letter he sent told all about his new little daughter. They named her Clarice. Clarice? What a name! I'll bet she weighs five thousand pounds."

"Hey, that's not like you, Pip. What'd your mom say? She must have dropped some bomb for you to be talking about your dad like that."

"It isn't any big deal."

"Really?"

"She's got some dude from Vermont coming in tonight on the train."

"That's why Mom's taking you to the program," John said. "I can't believe your mom's not coming to the program. She's had to listen to you banging on that piano for months. My mom's so tired of Christmas carols she's threatened me with all kinds of torture. This morning she said she was going to wire my braces together."

Pip smiled a little at John's joke.

"John, it's not that. Mom's coming to the program. The guy's coming, too. In fact, the guy's coming to everything. He's spending the holidays at our house."

"Oh," John said seriously. "I had that happen a few times on weekends. You get used to the idea. It's not so different from having a bunch of different fathers. Just stay in your room and leave them alone. If you go snooping around, you'll really catch it."

"I can't stay in my room," Pip said. "He's staying in it."

"Really? Well, that's not so bad after all. Your mom's really straight. She hasn't even brought a boyfriend to your place since your father left."

"I know. That's what has me so shook. She's never said anything about a man to me. Then all of a sudden she springs this on me. This guy's not just coming home. He's moving in."

"You think it's serious?"

"How do I know?"

"You'd better find out. Take it from me, new fathers are a pain. You spend a year staying out of their way. You spend another year figuring out what they want. Then when you're finally getting to know them, your mom sends them packing. What a headache!"

"Mom wouldn't do that," Pip said. "She plays for keeps. She waited five years for Dad to come back. She didn't even call a man. I listened to her cry at night. She was always telling me that my father would come back sometime and make everything right."

"Don't you think five years is long enough, Pip? I like your mom. Maybe this guy is right for her."

"Sure, and I'm Superman," Pip grumbled. "What's a guy old enough to be interested in Mom doing without a wife? I don't like the whole idea. He's going to hurt her. I just know it."

"You'd better jump back a step, Pip. If you try to mess things up, you'll end up being sorry. I tried to do something about number three, Mr. Humphrey. You remember him?"

"The one with the fat face?"

"Yeah, he's the one. If I hadn't messed around, Mr. Humphrey might have lasted. I never gave him a chance. I liked Zack Lewis, the guy before him. I just didn't give old Mr. Humphrey a chance, and he was the one that made Mom the happiest of all of them. Now she's just trapped with this Marshall guy. It won't last another year."

"How do you take it, John? Five fathers. Do any of them ever write or anything?"

"I see the real guy sometimes. He always sends me a Christmas present. But I figure a guy can raise himself once he's twelve, so I don't need too much of a father."

"Me, neither," Pip said. "I mean just listen to the guys in school griping about their fathers. Most of them would just as soon not have a father."

"Not if they spent a week without one," John said sadly. "I guess I'd give about anything to have a real good honest-to-God father."

"But you said . . ."

"I know, but you didn't mean what you said, either. It's fine to say it as long as you don't get to believing it too much."

"But it's such a big chance to take on a person, John. You know Linda Maxwell. She was so happy when her mom got married to that Mr. Kline. Now Linda can't stand the guy. They fight almost every night. She's about crazy over it. I don't have a dad, but Mom and I really have things together. We've got the chores all worked out, and she really helps me a lot. There are some times when I wish Dad was around, but this man may come in and ruin everything."

"That happens, Pip," John said. "But sometimes it happens the other way. Sometimes a really nice guy comes in and makes things work even better. Like Joey Keller. Joey got a new dad, and they go everywhere together. Now Joey has a little brother, too. They're really happy."

"All I need is a bunch of little brothers and sisters running around the house. I'd end up sharing my room with them, too."

"Babies grow up," John said. "Like my brothers. They're big enough to like nowadays."

"But by the time a kid got big enough to talk to, I'd be out of high school," Pip said. "I don't want a little brother. I don't want a new father. I just want things to be like they were yesterday."

"And your mom?"

"She's been fine all along."

"Has she?"

"You know I want the best for her. But I don't want to see her get involved with some dude and make a mistake. I don't want to have five fathers. I don't even want the one I have now."

"Take it from me, Pip. Give it a chance. Give them room. If you get someone you can live with, fine. But either way, if your mom likes him, if he makes her happy, then you have to give them a chance."

"Even if I'm not?" Pip asked.

"Wouldn't your mom be sad just to make you happy? Don't you think it's your turn?"

"I guess so," Pip said.

Pip could hardly wait for school to end that afternoon. He and the other members of the choir would walk the halls of the school singing Christmas carols they'd been practicing for weeks. Pip loved music better than anything else in the world, except for maybe his mother.

Pip played the piano part of the time. Mrs. Hewitt, the music teacher, let Pip and Elsie Nolan take turns accompanying the choir. It was a big thing to play in front of everyone, and Pip loved the extra attention.

He was good at singing, too. Pip was small for a seventh grader. He still wasn't quite five feet tall, and his thirteenth birthday wasn't all that far away. His bright blue eyes were a little too blue, a little too bright for anyone to think of him as being very old. His voice hadn't changed yet, so he could still hit the high notes people loved to hear from choirboys.

The song Pip loved best was "Silent Night." There were some special high notes in the song, and it was full of the holiday spirit. The one he had the most trouble with was "Deck the Halls." He and Jimmy Gaither had to sing with the girls on that one since most of the boys had deeper voices.

The choir gathered in the hall a few minutes before the end of the last class and then proceeded to walk through the halls singing.

When the bell finally rang for school to end, the little choir gathered in the music room. The other kids flew out the doors of the classrooms at full speed, throwing books, paper airplanes, pencils, hats, and whatever else they could to signal the beginning of the Christmas holidays.

"Phillip," Mrs. Hewitt said to Pip from the front of the room. "I'd like you to start us off with 'O Come All Ye Faithful.' Elsie, you will play 'Joy to the World.' Is that satisfactory?"

"My mother said she hoped I would have a chance to play the final song, Mrs. Hewitt," Elsie said. "I believe that's 'Silent Night.' "

"We will see," Mrs. Hewitt said. "Thank your mother for her interest, Elsie."

Pip smiled to himself. They all knew Elsie didn't play "Silent Night" half as well as Pip did.

Pip still had his mother on his mind that afternoon, though, and he missed three notes. Worse, he was confused by some notes of "Deck the Halls." More than anything else, he didn't want to be singing that song. But when it came to "Silent Night," he was ready. He hit the difficult chords of the new arrangement perfectly, and even Elsie agreed that Pip should play the piece.

"Elsie, Phillip, please stay," Mrs. Hewitt said when she dismissed the others.

"Yes, ma'am," the two of them said together.

"I'll get your books, Pip," John said, disappearing from the room.

"Children," Mrs. Hewitt said to them with a special smile. "I don't want you to be nervous tonight."

"I won't be," Elsie said. "I've had three recitals. I don't miss notes in front of people."

"I'll try to do better, ma'am," Pip said. "I've been kind of distracted today, but I'll be all right tonight."

"Good," Mrs. Hewitt said. "Phillip, I want you to start us off with 'Holy Night.' Then Elsie will do the others. We'll finish with 'Deck the Halls' and 'Silent Night.' You will play those."

"Thanks," Pip said to the woman, relieved.

"Thank you, Mrs. Hewitt," Elsie said.

"That's all, children," said Mrs. Hewitt.

Elsie scampered away, but Mrs. Hewitt stopped Pip for a moment.

"Phillip, is everything okay with you? You seem worried about something."

"I'll be all right tonight," he said. "Thanks for giving me a chance to play."

"You're not upset that Elsie is going to play most of the songs?"

"She should be playing all of them. I really fouled up today. I haven't had any recitals or anything, either."

"Is your mother going to come tonight, Phillip?"

"Yes, ma'am," he said. "She's bringing someone, too."

"Your father?"

"No ma'am," Pip said. "They're divorced."

"Is that what's got you upset?"

"No ma'am. They've been divorced for a long time."

"The other man, Phillip. The one she's bringing. Is that the problem?"

"I guess. I have to leave now, Mrs. Hewitt. John Mulligan is waiting. His mom will be mad if we're late."

"If you'd like to talk sometime, stop by," Mrs. Hewitt said.

"Thanks," Pip said, smiling at her. "It'll be fine. I'll play good tonight."

"Merry Christmas, Phillip."

"Merry Christmas, Mrs. Hewitt," he said, waving good-bye.

When Pip reached the parking lot, Mrs. Marshall was waiting. John was already in the car. Pip slid in alongside his friend, apologizing to Mrs. Marshall for being late.

"I understand musicians," Mrs. Marshall said. "I married a couple of them."

Mrs. Marshall laughed, but John scowled. Then the two boys worked feverishly to get Pip's green necktie tied around his neck so that his mother wouldn't find out it had been ditched after second period.

3

Pip had been waiting weeks for the night of the Christmas choir program. Nothing was as exciting as sitting in front of all the people and playing the piano. Even when he'd be singing, it would be a thrill to know that all the people in the audience were watching him, listening to the music he played or sang.

After an early dinner, Pip trotted back to his room and got out the simple white robe that served as the costume for the choir. His mother had washed and ironed the robe, and his name had been stitched in red over his heart.

"Phillip," it read.

Pip never used the name himself, but Mrs. Hewitt always called him Phillip, and it was the name that belonged on his choir robe. Pip slipped the robe over his shoulders and straightened it. Then he picked up a black tie and walked into the kitchen where his mother was putting the dishes away.

"I know it's a while before I have to leave, but I need your help."

"Help? What for, Pip?"

"With this," Pip said, waving the long black tie.

"Okay. Look, Pip, would you try it a couple of times by yourself. I'll be back to check on you in a minute."

"Thanks," he said, waving at her.

In the bathroom, the tie wasn't a bit cooperative. Pip got it tangled into a knot of the wrong sort. He unraveled it and started all over again. But when he was finished, it was still not a necktie knot.

"Having a little problem?" his mother asked, walking into the bathroom.

"Why can't I get it right, Mom?"

"That's a mighty heavy question, young man. But I think the answer lies here," she said, picking up his hands and squeezing them.

"What are you talking about?" Pip asked, pulling his hands away from her.

"It's an age-old problem," his mother said, laughing. "Your fingers are too little."

"Funny," Pip said, undoing the knot in the tie. "Now you try, Miss Fat Fingers."

"Fat fingers? I just might strangle you for that," she said, twisting the tie around his neck.

Pip pretended to be strangled, sticking out his tongue and rolling his eyes in imaginary pain.

"That's enough, Pip," his mother said. "Let's get you ready."

She took the two ends of the tie and magically wrapped one end around the other until it became a neatly formed knot. Then she took his brush and smoothed out the three strands of blond hair that fell across his eyes.

"Now, how's that, sir?" she asked, turning him to face the mirror.

"I look pretty good, huh?"

"Like a perfect gentleman. You're a little angel tonight, Pip."

"I wouldn't go that far," he said, his eyes twinkling with a trace of mischief. "A guy isn't supposed to be an angel. I might have a little trouble keeping that kind of an image up. Maybe I ought to put some ice cubes in my bed."

"We wouldn't want that," his mother said, laughing.

"We wouldn't?" Pip asked, smiling. "I guess not."

"Well, Pip," she said, putting her hands on his shoulders, "I have to go to the train station now. Will you be okay?"

"Sure, I'm not a little baby."

"You're quite a young man," she told him, giving him a hug. "You understand about Tom, don't you?"

"I guess so," Pip said. "You won't miss the program?"

"Not on your life. Be sure to thank Mrs. Marshall for the ride. Be polite, even to Elsie."

"I'll be polite," Pip sighed. "See you tonight, Mom."

"Good night, honey," she said, giving him a kiss.

Then she left, leaving Pip alone in the quiet of the December evening. Pip watched her car drive off and disappear down the street. When it was gone, he walked into the living room and sat down.

At six-thirty, Pip turned off the lights inside the house and slipped his heavy coat on over the light cotton choir robe. Then he walked outside, locked the door and trotted down the block to John Mulligan's house.

Mrs. Marshall was just walking out the door when Pip arrived.

"Right on time, Pip," the woman said. "Have you been practicing your piano playing?"

"I have the songs down pretty well," he said, sliding into the back seat next to John. "Is Mr. Marshall coming?"

"He has to do something tonight, Pip," John explained.

Then Mrs. Marshall started the engine, and they rode to the school in silence.

"Thanks for the ride, Mrs. Marshall," Pip told the woman as they got out of the car in the parking lot.

"You're always welcome," Mrs. Marshall said. "Now you boys get in there and knock 'em dead."

Pip and John raced across the parking lot and entered the building, laughing with excitement.

"What was that 'knock 'em dead' business?" Pip asked his friend.

"You know Mom," John said. "She still thinks she's an understudy on Broadway."

"Was she really in a big play in New York?"

"She tells everybody she was, but my grandmother told me she never got on stage. She should have. She's always acting out some part, mainly pretending she's a happy housewife. She likes to pretend she's a mother part of the time too."

"She isn't too bad a mother, John," Pip said.

"No, I guess not."

"She tries. That's about all you can expect."

"Yeah," John said. "Well, we'd better get onstage."

Pip and John then raced up the steps and made their way over to Mrs. Hewitt.

"Phillip," she said. "You'll take your place next to John Stephens. We've changed things a bit. You'll just play the last three songs. Be sure to stand on the end."

"But I'm too short to stand on the end," Pip protested.

"Look, Phillip," Mrs. Hewitt said. "You're going to play the last part of the program. If you're not on the end, you'll have to walk over half a dozen other children."

Pip winced every time she called them children.

"I understand," he told her.

Then he walked over and took his place on the end next to John Stephens.

The choir hunched together so that there would be room for everyone. Pip moved especially close to John Stephens. There was only about half an inch on the riser beyond his feet, and he didn't think the sight of him falling from the riser to his death was exactly how he wanted to be remembered that Christmas.

The choir stood perfectly still and quiet, waiting for the curtain to rise. Pip could hear the noise of the crowd already, and he was anxious for the program to begin. Elsie took her seat at the piano, and Mrs. Hewitt walked over and stood in front of them. The teacher nodded to the stage crew, and the curtain finally rose.

As the choir began singing "O Come All Ye Faithful," Pip looked out into the crowd for his mother. He searched one row of seats after another, but there was no sign of her or the strange man that she was supposed to be with.

Pip sang the song, but he lacked enthusiasm. His eyes no longer shined, and his chin fell to his chest. Not even a loud singing of "Joy to the World" lifted his spirits. When they finished the sixth song, Pip slipped down the edge of the risers and walked to the piano. Then he sat down at the piano bench and forced a smile across his face.

While Elsie rejoined the choir, Pip flipped through the pages of the music book until he came to "Holy Night." Then he glanced through the crowd one last time. As his eyes swept through the rear of the auditorium, he saw his mother walk in with a tall man with a moustache.

Pip watched them settle into two seats in the back of the auditorium. They sat down as if they belonged together, as if they were two parts of the same person. Before he had a chance to watch them anymore, though, Mrs Hewitt gave the signal for him to play, and his fingers danced across the piano keyboard, bringing the song to life.

Pip sang with a new spirit as he played. It was as if he could feel the warmth of his mother's eyes on his back. He didn't miss a single note. He even threw in a few complicated chords that brought new feeling to the songs.

When the choir finished singing, Pip turned the page of the music book to "Deck the Halls." He glanced out at the audience again, noticing that the man had his arm around his mother's back. They were talking softly, but Pip could tell his mother's eyes were watching the stage.

He felt better knowing she was watching him instead of the strange man at her side. When Mrs. Hewitt nodded to him, Pip began playing again. He didn't sing along with "Deck the Halls" since his high voice would stand out too much. It wasn't a long song, and soon the last notes rang out through the auditorium.

Mrs. Hewitt then turned to face the audience.

"I hope you have all enjoyed our performance," she told the people. "Christmas is a special time of the year, filled with joy and love. It is a time of sharing, a time of laughter, a time of peace. It is our hope that you will find in our last song the spirit of the season. We thank you for coming and sharing our celebration this night."

Then Mrs. Hewitt nodded to Pip, and the boy began the soft prelude to "Silent Night."

The song had always been a favorite of Pip's, and he did a special job on it that night. Every note seemed to sound brighter than ever before. And when Pip sang, he didn't hear any other voice except his own.

The choir was singing, too, though, and the audience was frozen by the beauty of the song. Some of the people smiled; others were close to tears. The young people themselves seemed caught up by the song, and their eyes were filled with emotion.

When Pip played the final notes, it seemed to him that the whole world echoed with that last line of the song.

"Sleep in heavenly peace."

But soon silence swept the stage, and Mrs. Hewitt dismissed the choir. Pip folded the music sheets into their case, then handed it over to Mrs. Hewitt.

"Merry Christmas, ma'am," he told her.

"Merry Christmas, Phillip," she said. "Who's the good-looking man with your mother?"

"His name is Tom something," Pip told her. "He's from Vermont."

"I hope you have a wonderful Christmas. You were very good tonight. The singing was fair, but the piano performance was extraordinary."

"Thank you, ma'am," Pip said, blushing. "I hope you have a good holiday."

"We will, Phillip. I'll see you after New Year's Day."

"Good-bye," Pip said, running to where John Mulligan was waiting.

"I can't stay long, Pip. Here's your coat," John said, handing it to Pip.

"Thanks, John. You coming over sometime?"

"Sure," John said. "I want to meet the tall guy with the moustache."

"Thanks a lot," Pip said, frowning. "I thought maybe we could watch some T.V."

"We can. I'll see you. Maybe tomorrow. Got to go, Pip. Merry Christmas."

"Merry Christmas," Pip said, waving good-bye to his friend.

Pip put on his coat and walked off the stage into the auditorium. His mother was waiting in the back, and Pip wove his way through the crowd to her.

"There he is," he heard his mother say. "He'll be here in a second, Tom."

Pip slowed down, trying to think of what to say. Then his mother pulled him to her side, and he stood face to face with the tall man.

"Tom," his mother said, "this is my son, Phillip."

"Good to see you, Phillip," the man said, shaking hands. "I've heard a great deal about you."

The man spoke in a slow manner, rounding his vowels to make them last longer.

"How are you, sir?" Pip asked. "I hope you had a good trip."

"A fine trip, Phillip. I really enjoyed listening to you play the piano. You're very good for a boy only eleven years old."

"I'm twelve and a half," Pip said firmly, frowning.

"I'm sorry, Phillip," the man said. "I heard someone say you were eleven. I should have remembered Ellen telling me you were twelve."

"It's all right."

"I really enjoyed your performance," the man told Pip. "It's the most I've enjoyed myself in months."

"They must not have much entertainment up in Vermont, huh?" Pip asked. "Choir programs aren't too thrilling."

"Well, you all were very good tonight," his mother said. "I haven't heard some of the chords you put in tonight. Have you been practicing at school?"

"I wanted to surprise you, Mom."

"You did. Well, are you ready to go home?"

"Sure," Pip said.

"I've never ridden in a car with a fine musician before," Tom told Pip as they walked to the car.

"I'm not a fine musician, sir. I'm just learning."

"Philip, I'm not used to being called sir. Would you do me the favor of calling me Tom?"

Pip saw the plea in his mother's eyes. He swallowed his wish to refuse and gave in.

"Okay, Tom," Pip mumbled.

"I can tell we're going to be great friends," Tom said, putting a large hand on Pip's shoulder.

Pip slipped out of the man's grasp and looked up into Tom's surprised eyes. Pip didn't say anything, but he'd pretty well summed up how it would be. Pip didn't need another friend or another father. Tom might as well know that from the start.

4

When Pip's mother pulled the car into the driveway, he scrambled out and raced to open the garage door. Then the car slid into its place, and Pip closed the door behind them.

"Pip, why don't you help Tom with his suitcases?" his mother suggested. "You can show him the house, too, if you'd like."

Pip took the car keys and opened the trunk. Tom took two of the suitcases, and Pip took a strange metal case and an overnight bag. Leading the way inside, Pip turned to Tom.

"It's this way," Pip sighed, motioning the way to his room.

"You're the guide, Phillip," Tom told him. "I'll follow you.'

Pip dragged himself down the hall and opened the door to his room.

"I moved some stuff out of the closet," Pip explained. "There's room for you to hang up anything you want."

"Thank you, Phillip," Tom said. "That was nice of you."

"Mom told me to," Pip said, frowning. "I also took everything out of the top drawer of the dresser. I guess you can find everything all right."

"I'll manage," Tom said. "I really appreciate you giving up your room for me. I know it's kind of a tough thing not having your own room at Christmas, but I know we'll be good friends. Whenever you need something, just come in and get it. I grew up in a large family, and I'm used to little brothers and nephews all over the place at Christmas."

"I wouldn't know about any of that," Pip said, grumbling to himself as he left the room.

Pip found his mother rolling out dough in the kitchen. Every Christmas she made batches of cookies in all sorts of holiday shapes.

"I thought you were going to show Tom the house," she said as he picked up a cookie cutter shaped like a bell.

"You said if I wanted to," he reminded her. "I don't. I don't even want him here."

"Remember your promise, young man. You know these cookies are for you. John Mulligan would be a little upset if he came over here and there were no Christmas cookies for the two of you to get sick on."

"I'm not in the way, am I?"

"Yes," she said, walking over and putting a ball of dough on his nose. "Why don't you go get into some other clothes. You can entertain Tom while I get the baking done."

"Okay," Pip sighed. "What should I put on?"

"Are you sleepy?" she asked.

"Not really."

"Then put on a pair of jeans and a shirt. How about one of your jerseys? They're good and warm."

"Okay," Pip said, stumbling his way to his room to get the other clothes.

Pip knocked lightly on the open door of his room.

"Come in," Tom said, glancing around.

"I have to change clothes," Pip said. "I just need to grab some stuff. Sorry to bother you."

"You're not a bother, Phillip," Tom said, walking toward him. "It's going to be nice to be with you. I don't get a chance to spend time with kids much."

"I'm not a kid," Pip told him.

"Well, I'm glad to be around you anyway."

"Sure," Pip said, finding the clothes and grabbing his pajamas as well. "See you later," Pip added, slipping out of the room and walking down the hall to the bathroom.

It took only a few minutes for Pip to peel off his choir robe and good clothes. Then he pulled on his jeans and slipped a football jersey over his shoulders. Dressed, he put the robe and his slacks on hangers, dropped the white shirt into the dirty clothes hamper and stumbled out of the bathroom. He stopped to hang up his clothes in the hall closet. Then he walked into the living room and sat down on the sofa.

Tom walked in a few seconds later and sat down beside him.

"Do you play football, Phillip?" Tom asked.

"I played baseball last year," Pip mumbled. "I have a bunch of football jerseys. My grandfather sends them.

I guess I like football okay. I throw the ball around with my friends some, but I don't play on a regular team."

"Why not?"

"You played football when you were my age, right? That's what everybody says. A guy doesn't have to play football, you know."

"You might try it, though. I never played football. In Vermont, kids play hockey most of the time. I was a hockey player. That and basketball. Since you play baseball, you know it's fun to play on a team."

"Sometimes," Pip said, moving to the edge of the sofa. "I don't play football 'cause I'm too small. I'd get crunched. I've been thinking about playing soccer next year. John Mulligan and John Stephens play soccer."

"That sounds like it would be fun," Tom said.

Pip rested his chin on his small hand and frowned. For five minutes utter silence filled the room. Then Tom coughed.

"Tell me about yourself, Phillip," the man said. "What do you like to do?"

"I don't know," Pip said.

"You play the piano. And very well. Would you play something for me?"

"Mom's baking. Besides, I'm tired of playing."

"Maybe another time."

"Maybe."

Tom looked around the room a couple of times.

"Is that you on the wall?" Tom asked.

"The kid with the long blond hair?" Pip asked.

"In the sailor suit. Is that your father with you?"

"Yes," Pip sighed. "That was the last year we were together. I was five then."

"You were a nice looking boy. You've become an even better looking young man."

"Thanks. You want to look at my yearbook? It's the one from last year when I was just a sixth grader."

"I'd enjoy that," Tom said.

Pip walked over to the bookshelf and picked up the small white book. Then he carried it over and handed it to Tom.

"Are you listed by grade?" Tom asked.

"Yeah. I'm in the first part."

"Here you are, Phillip Edwin North. You haven't changed much."

"I know. I still look like a sixth grader. You thought I was eleven, remember?"

"Phillip, you're not too small to be twelve. Lots of boys don't start growing until they're fourteen or fifteen."

"Don't say that. I couldn't stand being a little guy for another two whole years."

"Well, I'm not a fortune teller, but it seems to me you're not too small. You'll probably start growing any day now."

"You think so?"

"Sure," Tom said, smiling at Pip.

Pip just frowned. Then he put away the yearbook and sat down in a chair on the other side of the room.

"What do you usually do around Christmas time?" Tom asked. "Do you sing Christmas carols? Watch television?"

"I usually put the decorations on the tree," Pip said. "We don't even have a tree this year."

"Who usually gets the tree? Do you have an artificial one, or do you buy an evergreen?"

"Dad used to pick up a pine tree after work. Lately Mom and I've gone and picked one out."

"Get your coat, Phillip Edwin North," Tom said, standing up. "We're going to go pick out the prettiest fir tree you've ever seen."

"I don't know about that," Pip said.

"Get your coat. I'll tell your mother we're going."

"Okay," Pip said, walking to the closet to get his coat.

A few minutes later Pip raised the garage door and waited for Tom to pull the car out onto the driveway. When the car was clear, Pip closed the garage door and slid into the front seat across from Tom.

"Getting chilly," Tom told him, shaking Pip's shoulder. "Reminds me of Christmas in Vermont."

"I guess it snows up there."

"Deep enough to swallow small boys," Tom said, his voice filling with excitement. "My dad has a nice little farm, about fifty acres of rolling hillside outside the Green Mountains. In the winter the countryside is white with snow. The snow gathers in the tree branches, all white and pure and cold.

"When I was a boy, my brother Tim and I used to pick out the Christmas tree. We didn't go down to a lot where some merchant sold them as you do. We walked out into the hills with our sled and marked a tree. Then we came back near Christmas and cut it down."

"You cut down your own tree?" Pip asked.

"Yes. Then while Tim loaded the tree onto the sled,

I'd climb a beech tree and cut down a nice cluster of mistletoe."

"Mistletoe grows in the high branches of oak trees down at the park," Pip said. "We sometimes climb up and get pieces of it to sell."

Tom turned the car down Lakeside Avenue, heading toward Grand Avenue.

"Once we got the tree back to the house," Tom continued "we'd set it up in the living room. My mother and sisters would bake fudge and cookies. My father would bring down a box of silver bells and shiny stars, brightly painted balls and little wooden soldiers, and strings of beads and glass. There wasn't one store-bought item that touched that tree. It was a beautiful Christmas tree, Phillip."

"It sounds fantastic."

"And in the evenings we'd gather around the piano and sing Christmas carols. On Christmas Eve, we'd meet at the village church and ski across the hills, holding lanterns in our hands. It was like a chain of light dancing across the horizon. There's no sight on this earth prettier than those lights glimmering off the snowbanks."

"We don't get snow too often in Texas," Pip said sadly. "It snowed a little a couple of weeks ago, but there's never enough snow to go skiing."

"Maybe sometime I'll take you to Vermont to spend Christmas with my family. You'd like them, Phillip. I have three nephews your age."

Pip wanted to smile, but he wouldn't give in. Instead he wrinkled his forehead and frowned.

"I don't see how I could go to Vermont," Pip said.

"Mom doesn't like me to stay away for more than a few hours."

"Maybe the three of us could go together," Tom said.

"I don't think so," Pip said, sighing. "Hey, there's a place over on the right. Stop!" Pip cried, pointing to a Christmas tree stand.

Tom pulled the car into a small parking lot. Then the two of them stepped out into the cold.

"I see a nice tree," Pip said, walking over to a small cedar tree.

"That's a nice tree for a cedar," Tom said, "but I promised you the grandest tree you've ever seen. Let's go over and find a Douglas fir."

"They're very expensive. Mom always picks out a cedar."

"This is my project, Phillip. A Douglas fir it must be. Come along, son."

"I'm not your son," Pip said, stopping.

"Sorry," Tom said, a frown crossing his face.

Then they walked back into the trees. Tom knew trees well, and he picked out a tall Douglas fir that dwarfed all the others.

"That tree's as big as a house," Pip said.

"Too big?" Tom asked him.

"Is there any such thing? I never heard of too big a Christmas tree."

Pip smiled at the man for the first time, and Tom took him by the shoulder and led him to the saleswoman.

"We've chosen a tree," Tom said. "I'd like to give you twenty-five dollars for it."

"Yes, sir," the woman said, following them to the

tree. "But, sir, that tree is marked at thirty-five dollars. I can't sell it for twenty-five."

"Well, you do what you must," Tom said. "I won't pay more than twenty-five for a tree this late in the season. You'll just end up burning it for firewood."

"Well, sir," the woman said. "I suppose twenty-five is a fair price. It's a deal."

Pip looked at Tom's sneaky smile. This was an unusual man.

The two of them took the giant tree and loaded it into the back of the car. Then they drove back home, humming Christmas carols along the way.

When they got the tree inside, Pip's mom was amazed.

"That's the most enormous tree I've ever seen," she said. "You must have paid a small fortune."

"Tom talked the lady at the Christmas tree place into letting him have it for ten dollars under the price," Pip told her.

"Well, it appears you've had quite a fine time together," Pip's mom said, hugging the two of them. "Get out of your coats and let's get this tree decked out."

"Yes, ma'am," Pip said, running to the closet to put his coat away.

Tom helped Pip's mother get the boxes of ornaments down from the attic, and Pip set the tree stand in its corner of the living room. Then the three of them swung the heavy tree into its stand and filled the tray with water and sugar.

His mother set up a ladder, and Pip hung the bright star on the top of the tree. Then his mother went back to her baking, and Tom helped Pip decorate the tree with lights and tinsel. Then they hung the ornaments. As they worked, Tom spoke softly about Vermont and snow and Christmas. Then he turned seriously to Pip.

"Tell me, Phillip, why does your mother call you Pip?"

"It's a nickname," Pip explained, hanging a silver bell on a branch of the tree.

"How'd you get it?"

"My dad gave it to me. I was about four years old. I used to go in and sit on his lap at night. He'd hold me against him and pat me on the head. Then he'd tell me stories. One time he told me a story about a boy named Phillip. It was from a book, and in the book, this Phillip could never say his whole name. He could only say Pip."

"Was there a convict in the story?"

"Yes," Pip said. "And Pip lived with his brother-in-law because his father and mother were dead. His brother-in-law was a blacksmith named Joe."

"The book was written by an Englishman named Charles Dickens. It's called *Great Expectations*. It was one of my favorites when I was a boy. Have you read anything by Dickens?"

"I read *Oliver Twist* for a book report," Pip said. "We read *A Christmas Carol* in English last week. He writes about old times."

"They weren't old times when he wrote about them. He died a hundred years ago."

"That long ago? Anyway, Dad started calling me Pip after that. Mom picked it up. That's what she's called me ever since. I like the name. I guess it's because it's about all I have left of Dad."

"Do you miss him?"

"Not really," Pip said. "It doesn't really matter. I do fine."

"Don't you miss having a man around to play catch with?"

"I play catch with John Mulligan. I do all right," Pip said, glancing away as he put the last of the ornaments on the tree.

"Would you like to see what Pip would have looked like?" Tom asked him, pointing toward the sofa. "I can draw him for you, Phillip."

"Can you?"

"Let me get my drawing board," Tom said, disappearing for a moment.

Tom walked back in and sat down beside Pip. Pip watched as the figure of a boy took shape on the drawing pad. The boy wore a dark coat and knee britches, with buckles on his shoes. He stood with bright eyes and light hair partially covered by a black top hat. Pip watched as Tom drew three strands of hair falling across the boy's eyes.

"That's a fine drawing," Pip said, trying not to sound excited.

"It's my craft," Tom said. "It's also my hobby, just like yours is playing the piano. Drawing brings a man peace."

"Sure."

"You two men finished with the tree?" his mother asked. "It's time Pip was in bed."

"Mom, I need some sheets," Pip said.

"They're on the ironing board," she told him. "Can you make up the sofa by yourself?"

"I can do anything by myself," Pip said, glancing at Tom.

His mother and Tom left the room, and Pip made the sofa into a bed. Then he went into the bathroom and changed into his pajamas. Ready for bed, he slipped under the blankets and pulled them tight against his chin.

Pip looked around him at the room. It was too silent. He could hear his mother laughing in the other part of the house. Then she walked in and sat down on the sofa beside him.

"Good night, Pip," she said, kissing him. "Sleep snug and tight."

"Good night, Mom," Pip said.

As she walked away, Pip's eyes grew heavy, and sleep captured him.

5

Pip woke around six o'clock. It was unusual for him to stir so early, especially on a Saturday. But the Christmas season has a way of doing strange things to people, and so Pip scrambled to his feet.

He yawned away a last trace of sleepiness, then listened for the voices of his mother and Tom. The house was filled with silence, though, so Pip tiptoed his way across the living room and walked down the hall to his bedroom.

Pip stopped outside the door and listened carefully for any noise. He shivered with cold, and his bare feet felt as though they were frozen to the floor. Then he opened the door and sneaked quietly inside.

Pip paused a moment when he got inside. He looked at the bed where Tom was sleeping peacefully. The sheets covered the man's slender waist, but Tom's bare chest was exposed. Even asleep it was clear that he was powerfully built. That was the way Pip wanted to look, all tall and strong. Pip was amazed at the dark curly hair that covered the man's chest.

Something uneasy filled Pip's insides as he tiptoed over to the dresser. He opened the middle drawer and took out some clean clothes. As Pip started to leave, he heard a noise behind him.

"Good morning," Tom said, sitting up in bed.

"Good morning, sir," Pip said, feeling embarrassed. "I didn't mean to disturb you. I was just getting some clean clothes."

"You didn't disturb me. I'm a morning man myself. Is your mother up yet?"

"I don't think so."

"Just us men, huh? Well, how about sitting down and keeping me company for a few minutes?"

Pip sat nervously on the edge of the bed. Tom sat up and put a hand on the boy's shoulder.

"Would you mind me asking a favor of you?" Tom asked.

"I guess not."

"Would you be upset if I called you Pip?"

"No," Pip said. "It's what people call me."

"I'd like to think I'm a little more than just people, I've grown kind of fond of you. You remind me an awful lot of myself when I was your age."

"I'll bet you were never small."

"It's not size that counts, Pip. It's what's inside."

"What's inside me?"

"Something special," Tom said. "You notice everything. You're always looking around at things. And when you feel strongly about something, you stick to it."

"Huh?"

"You're very loyal, Pip, even to your father."

"Not to him," Pip said, frowning. "He doesn't even

write. I send him letters, but he never writes back. Well, he had his chance. I'm not going to write again. He'll be sorry one of these days."

"He will be, too. He doesn't know how proud he should be."

"Sure."

"You let it bother you too much, though. A man can't be worrying about things he can't change."

"I guess not."

"Tell me something. How do you feel about me? Honestly, okay?"

"You're all right."

"But you'd just as soon I weren't here."

"Mom wants you here," Pip said, squirming. "She hasn't brought anyone home since Dad went away. She likes you."

"I like her, too."

"I love her," Pip said. "I worry about her."

They sat together in silence for a minute. Then Pip turned to Tom with a serious face.

"You like her a lot, don't you?" Pip asked the man.

"As much as I've liked anyone in a long time. I've been pretty lonely lately. I grew up with people all around me. It was always hard finding time to be alone, to do what I wanted to do. I promised myself that when I got out of college, I'd see the world, do things. Then somehow I got used to being by myself. It isn't the way I like to be, Pip. People need other people."

"You need Mom, huh?"

"That's the way it is."

Pip thought to himself that his mom needed Tom, too. He couldn't bring himself to say it out loud, though.

"You sure have a lot of hair on your chest," Pip said, staring at the man. "I guess that happens when you get to be old."

"Well, Pip," Tom said, laughing. "I don't think I'm so old."

"I didn't mean to say something stupid. I was only wondering."

"It's only natural to ask questions," Tom said, patting Pip on the back. "I'll bet you can answer your own question, though. Haven't you seen other men with their shirts off? What about your father?"

"I don't remember Dad," Pip said with a frown. "I guess I've seen some men that didn't have hair all over their chests."

"Well, some men do and others don't," Tom said. "I don't know why. I never thought about it much. I guess it's just the same way some men are tall and others are short."

"I don't remember if Dad was tall or short. I don't think he was as tall as you are."

"You know, the size of a man or the hair on his chest doesn't make him a better man or a lesser one. It's what's inside a man that makes him what he is."

"But I don't remember anything about him," Pip said, looking away. "I don't even remember how he sounded."

"Don't you talk to him on the phone?"

"No," Pip said, swallowing hard.

"It's all right," Tom said, moving closer. "It isn't anything that should trouble you."

"I guess not," Pip said.

"Say, have you ever been tickled? I mean, really tickled?"

"Don't!" Pip said, trying to pull away from him.

Tom was too quick and too strong, though, and he had Pip squealing and laughing in no more than a second. Pip thrashed and rolled on the floor and begged to be released, but the man kept tickling him in his skinny ribs. Finally Tom released him, and they laughed at each other.

"I haven't laughed so much in a year," Tom said.

"That's 'cause you were having all the fun," Pip said, trying to frown.

But the good feeling that was flowing through Pip's insides forced a smile out.

"What would you say to getting dressed and going into the kitchen? Your mom will be up soon, and we'll have some breakfast."

"I'll see you," Pip said. He walked to the bathroom and got dressed.

When Pip was dressed, he smoothed out his hair and walked into the kitchen. His mother was cooking breakfast, and the ham and eggs brought his hungry stomach to life.

"Mom, when's breakfast?" Pip asked.

"Just a few more minutes," she said, smiling at him. "I understand you and Tom had a nice talk this morning."

"We talked some," Pip said.

"Let's talk some more," Tom said, sitting down at the table across from Pip.

"What about?" Pip asked.

"How about the last Christmas you spent with your dad. What did the two of you do?"

"We put together some electric trains," Pip said.

"I had some trains when I was small. I'll always

remember my father and I building a big mountain out of papier-mâché. We made a little station out of wood and painted lakes and rivers on a plywood board. We added trees and cabins and people. I remember my brother Tim and I making a church and a little schoolhouse. It was one of my favorite Christmases."

"I'd like to do that sometime."

"Did you ever want anything else at Christmas?"

"Lots of things," Pip said. "I always wanted some toy soldiers. My dad promised to get me some a couple of years ago. I remember him reading to me about a toy soldier that was in love with a ballerina."

"That was the fairy tale about the steadfast tin soldier," Tom said.

"You know a lot of stories."

"My mother loved to read," Tom told him. "She used to read to us when it was too cold to do anything else."

"I never wanted tin soldiers, though," Pip explained. "I wanted some wooden ones. I saw some once in a store. They wore bright red uniforms with black pants and white straps across their chests."

"Like British soldiers," Tom said. "Have you ever considered blue coats? That way they'd be Americans."

"That would have been okay. Even purple would have been all right. But he never sent them. He promised, but they never came."

"And a promise is for keeps, right, Pip?" his mother asked, bringing the breakfast to them on a big platter.

"Right, Mom," Pip said.

6

Pip helped his mother with the breakfast dishes. She cleared the table while he rinsed the plates. Then he loaded the dishwasher. When he finished, he heard the engine of the car roar into action in the garage.

"Mom?" he called out.

"Right here," his mother answered, walking back into the kitchen.

"Where's Tom going?" Pip asked.

"I don't know," she told him. "He just said there was something he'd forgotten to do. Then he borrowed the car keys and dashed outside."

"He's kind of strange, isn't he?" Pip asked, laughing.

"I don't think so," she said, sitting down at the table. "Why did you say that?"

"This morning I woke him up. I mean if some little kid woke me up on a Saturday, I would have yelled or hit him or something. He just sat up and talked to me."

"About what?"

"Lots of things," Pip said, walking over and sitting down at the table across from her.

"Like what?"

"We talked about Dad. We talked about you, too."

"Anything else?"

"Hairy chests," Pip said, laughing. "And he tickled me. I tell you, Mom, watch out for those fingers of his. They can really tickle a guy. I thought I was going to die."

"And you didn't mind?"

"No," Pip said, a puzzled look coming to his face. "I don't know why, either. I don't like him very much. I don't know why I didn't kick him or something. It's what I would have done yesterday."

"Do you suppose you didn't kick him for the same reason he didn't get mad when you woke him? Do you suppose it's because you two kind of like each other?"

"It couldn't be that. I must have been too sleepy or something."

"You sure?"

"Positive," Pip said. "There's no way. It must have been 'cause I was confused about all the things he said."

"Must have been," his mother said, smiling. "Thank you, Pip," she added, hugging him.

"For what?" he asked, pulling away from her. "Boy, people sure are acting strange around here."

"You go brush your hair, young man," his mother told him.

Pip walked into the bathroom and brushed his hair back into shape. Then he walked into the living room and turned on the television. As the beginning of an old movie flashed onto the screen, Pip folded up his sheets and blankets and put them in the hall closet. Then he straightened up the room and switched on the Christmas tree lights.

The movie was over at eleven, and the doorbell rang. Pip glanced around to see if his mom would answer it. When she failed to appear, he trotted over and opened the door.

"Hi, Pip," said John Mulligan, his bright face half-covered by a huge knit cap and woolen scarf.

"You want to come in or play outside?" Pip asked.

"Is 'he' here?" John asked.

"No," Pip answered, opening the door. "Inside, huh?"

"It's pretty cold out there today. I think we'd better do something inside."

"I have a jigsaw puzzle of the space shuttle. My grandfather sent it. I've never put it together. You want to try it?"

"Sure, Then when it warms up, we can go out and toss the football. Okay?"

"Okay with me," Pip said, walking to his room to get the puzzle.

Pip and John got out the card table and began putting the puzzle together. First they separated all the outside pieces and put them together. Then Pip started putting together the pieces of the earth while John worked on the white pieces of the shuttle.

"It's really going to be neat to be out of school for ten whole days," John said, fitting a new piece together.

"Holidays never last long enough. And it's not too neat to have Christmas without snow. It snows up North all the time."

"We had a bunch of snow a few years ago. You can't

expect snow every year. That's why they call this the Sun Belt. It's sunny."

"It isn't fair to have no snow on Christmas, though. Tom was telling me about how they have Christmas in Vermont. They have loads of snow. They pick out their own Christmas trees and cut them down. They ski down the sides of mountains with lanterns swinging in their hands. They put mistletoe all over the place."

"I thought you didn't like him," John said.

"I don't. I was only telling you how they have Christmas up where he's from."

"Sounds to me like you'd rather be up there."

"I was just saying I'd like some snow down here."

"But you'd rather be up there cutting down your own tree."

"Well, I'd like to see new places. I'd like to go anywhere I haven't been."

"It's nice to be out of school, anyway. Have you got your book picked out for Mrs. Curry's book report?"

"I read it last week."

"I hate guys like you," John said, frowning. "You can read a book in a flash, and you play the piano better than Elsie Nolan. If you could play football, you'd be too much to take."

"I can't spell," Pip said.

"That's right. That keeps you from being the perfect seventh grader. You have to sing 'Deck the Halls' with the girls, too. I guess I can stand you for a friend."

"I was really worrying," Pip said, rolling his eyes. "You can't be too picky about your friends, you know."

"I'm not exactly a genius myself, am I?"

"Not exactly," Pip said, laughing at his friend. "Have you seen Brenda Simpson's new hairdo?"

"It looks like she got caught in a frizzie factory. I liked her better when her hair was straight. She's got so many curls in it now you'd think she was a commercial for a Shirley Curly doll or something."

"Yeah," Pip said, laughing with his friend.

"Say, what do you suppose Carol Johnson will do next? She's been giving you some pretty heavy eye contact lately."

"She'll probably grow three inches over the holidays," Pip said with a frown. "That'll mean there won't be a single girl in the seventh grade who isn't taller than me."

"That would be a disaster," John said. "I can see you dancing in the gym with Joan Harmeyer."

"Pip and the beast," Pip said, laughing until his face turned red. "She's almost six feet tall."

"She could play for the Rams. She's bigger than their quarterback."

"I heard she was holding out for a contract with the circus. They need a new freak."

"She's not a freak. Just tall. She's really pretty nice."

"Giving up on Gail Burnett?" Pip asked, elbowing his friend.

"Knock it off. Gail and I are almost steadies."

"How almost?"

"Well, I haven't asked her. When I get up the nerve, she'll say yes."

"You sure?"

"I'm sure. John Stephens told me. His sister and Gail are best friends."

"Sara Stephens is an authority," Pip said seriously. "There can be no doubt."

"Okay," John said, putting the space shuttle pieces where they belonged. "Now let's get the sky together."

Pip put the earth pieces in and the two of them set to filling in the few blank spots remaining. It took them only about thirty minutes. Then they looked with admiration at their work.

"We ought to frame it," John said.

"It looks good. Ready?" Pip asked.

John nodded. Then they ripped the puzzle apart, dumping the pieces back into the box.

"You want to toss the football now?" John asked.

"On the way to the park," Pip told his friend. "I need something there."

"At the park? What?"

"You remember the big oak trees in the park? There's mistletoe in the top branches."

"I know that. Sam Crandell used to climb those trees and sell the stuff."

"This year I'm climbing the trees."

"To sell the mistletoe?"

"No, John. So we'll have a real Christmas. Tom bought that huge tree," Pip explained, pointing to the tree. "It's up to me to get the mistletoe."

"But the mistletoe's a long ways up there," John reminded him. "You don't like to climb trees."

"I'll manage. Come on."

The two boys raced each other to the park, flipping the football along the way. When they arrived at the oak trees, Pip looked up through the naked branches at the mistletoe.

"It's a long ways, Pip," John told him.

"Not so long," Pip said. "Give me a boost."

"Okay," John said, putting the football down long enough to help his friend up the tree. "Get some for my mom, too."

"Sure," Pip said.

Pip didn't particularly like heights, but he climbed the tree anyway. He wanted that mistletoe more than he wanted anything else in the world right then, so nothing could get in the way. When Pip set his mind to something, it usually got done.

Pip struggled his way up the old tree, scraping his hands and chin on the branches. He pulled himself up slowly, curling his legs around the branches to keep from falling. When he finally reached the first cluster of mistletoe, half the people in the park were yelling to him to cut down some for them, too. Pip took off two nice clusters for himself and Mrs. Marshall. Then he tore the rest loose and let it fall to the ground. While the people divided up the mistletoe and cheered him, Pip crawled his way back to the ground.

"You were great, Pip," John told him, taking the mistletoe. "Thanks."

"Anytime," Pip said. "Only next year you climb the tree."

"Deal," John said, tossing the football to Pip.

The two of them laughed and ran their way back to the house. Then they set down the mistletoe and threw the football around.

"Hi," said Tom, walking out to watch them. "Mind if I give it a try?"

Pip nodded to John, and John threw the ball to Tom.

"Go out for a pass, Pip," Tom said.

Pip looked at John for a minute, then raced down the street. After Pip ran about thirty yards, Tom fired the ball. Pip ran under it. The ball was there, but it bounced off Pip's hands.

Pip kicked the ground and picked up the ball. Then the boys ran back to Pip's yard.

"That was a great pass, mister," John said. "I never saw a guy throw a ball that far."

"It was my fault," Pip said, looking at the ground. "I dropped it."

"You want to try it again?" Tom asked.

"We're kind of tired," Pip said, handing the football to John. "Maybe another time. You want some hot chocolate, John?"

"Sure," John said, following Pip inside.

"You want some, too?" Pip asked Tom.

"Okay," Tom told him, smiling.

Pip walked into the kitchen and heated some hot water. When the kettle boiled, Pip poured in the cocoa mix and returned with three cups of chocolate.

"Who's your friend?" Tom asked Pip.

"This is John Mulligan," Pip said.

"I thought the only thing called Mulligan was stew," Tom said, laughing. "That sounds like a name from an English novel."

"No," John said. "There are a lot of real live Mulligans. I went to a reunion last year at Grandmother Mulligan's house. There were big Mulligans, little Mulligans, even medium-sized Mulligans. Mulligans all over the place."

"I stand corrected," Tom said. "I'm Tom Paxton, a friend of Pip's mother."

"Glad to meet you," John said, shaking the man's hand. "Well, I'd better get going. Mom gets mad if I stay too long. See you, Pip. Nice to meet you, Mr. Paxton."

"It's Tom," the man said.

"Sure," John told him. "Good-bye."

"Bye," Pip said, walking with John to the door.

7

Pip spent the rest of the afternoon hanging the mistletoe around the house. He put one cluster over the front door, a second around a Christmas candle his mother had placed over the fireplace, and a third over the kitchen door. When his mother and Tom walked into the dining room, they looked at the mistletoe and stopped in their tracks.

"Where did this come from?" his mother asked.

"I climbed the oak tree in the park and got it," Pip said. "Tom told me about how they used to cut down their own trees and put mistletoe all over the place. I thought since he got the tree, I should get the mistletoe."

"I think that was very nice of you," his mother told him.

"Thank you, Pip," Tom said. "It's beginning to seem like home around here."

Tom put his arm around Pip's mother, giving her a hug. Pip frowned at them, then walked into the kitchen.

"Hey, just a minute there," his mother called to him. "You just passed under the mistletoe. Who do you want to kiss you?"

"What?" Pip said. "Men don't get kissed by other men. Besides, it only works if you're both under the mistletoe."

"Not where I come from," his mother said. "What'll it be?"

"Okay," Pip said, turning his cheek up toward her. "I sure don't want *him* to do it."

His mother gave him a soft kiss, then hugged him.

"Pip, we were just joking with you," she whispered. "I wish you wouldn't keep calling Tom 'him,' I wish you'd try to be a little more friendly."

"I didn't promise that," Pip whispered back to her. "I never promised to let him be my new dad."

"I didn't ask you to," she said. "Just try not to be so cold to him. He cares about you. He went out to buy that tree last night so you'd have one."

"He did that for you, Mom," Pip said.

"For you," she said, softly squeezing his shoulder the way she always did when she wanted him to know she loved him. "I've never asked you for anything in your whole life. Please, Pip, be nice to Tom."

"Okay," Pip sighed.

At dinner the three of them talked about holidays and music and people. Pip sat on one side of the table while his mom and Tom sat together on the other side. As they ate, Pip studied the looks on their faces. His mother's eyes were full of laughter. She seemed to smile at everything Tom said. Pip had never seen her so happy.

Pip didn't know what to make of Tom. The man's eyes were all aglow, and his mouth was always open in a kind of laughing smile.

But Pip didn't need to look at their faces to see what

they were thinking and how they felt. He watched Tom's hand wrap around his mother's waist, and he saw her lean her shoulder against the man. It was love all right, no doubt about it. They were acting too silly for it to be anything else. They laughed at things that weren't funny, and they smiled when they should have been enjoying their dinner.

Mom should have another man, Pip thought to himself. She had a right to be happy. But Pip couldn't convince himself he really wanted a second father. He felt a nervous shiver run down his spine, and a plot hatched in his brain to do all he could to break them up.

Then he remembered his promise, and he shook his head. He felt guilty for wanting to spoil his mother's happiness. There had been plenty of times when she'd set aside her wishes so Pip could be happy. It was time it worked the other way around.

"You seem lost in some very deep thoughts, Pip," his mother said to him as she passed a bowl of mashed potatoes. "What are you thinking about?"

"Nothing," Pip said, hiding the lie that was written all over his face.

"Pip, what do you usually do two days before Christmas Eve?" Tom asked.

"Nothing," Pip said. "Mom and I usually go shopping. I have most of my presents, though, and I don't think she wants to go shopping tonight."

"Good thinking," his mother said. "We'll go out Monday if you need something."

"That's Christmas Eve," Pip said. "The stores will be swamped."

"Then you should have gone out with Tom this morning," his mother said.

"You went shopping?" Pip asked. "How come?"

"I forgot to bring some things down with me from Boston," Tom said. "Always remember to pack your toothbrush, Pip."

"I never go anywhere," Pip mumbled.

"I figure you will," Tom said. "You look like an explorer to me."

"He's going to be a concert pianist," his mother said. "Mrs. Hewitt says he has a great future as a musician."

"She only says that because she doesn't know much about piano players," Pip said. "I think I'd like to be an astronaut maybe. That or a geologist."

"Things sure have changed," Tom said. "When I was twelve, I wanted to be a railroad engineer. I remember that every year about Christmas time my father would go out to the storage shed and get out the crate that had my trains in it."

"Did you set them up?" Pip asked. "Even the mountains and the lakes you painted? And the little town and all the people?"

"That's the way it was," Tom told him. "It took us about half an hour to set up the track and the little village. Then the whole family would settle around the track, and I would start the trains going.

"I had this small railroad engineer's cap that some uncle had sent me, and I'd run the trains through the tunnels, over the mountain, into the station. Whenever I'd pump my hand, my sister Anne would let out a terrible whistle."

"How many trains did you have?" Pip asked.

"I had three engines," Tom said, his mouth broadening into a smile. "I could run two entire trains at one time."

"I never had but one train," Pip said sadly.

"That's right," Pip mother said. "Pip had an electric train. His father gave it to him several years ago."

"I was only a little kid then. I loved that train," Pip said, trembling. "Dad would sit there and hold me in his lap. He'd let me work the throttle. It really felt great to run that train."

"You don't run it anymore?" Tom asked.

"I get it out and look at it. I climb up to the attic when I'm lonely sometimes, and I clean all the cars. But I don't run it. Not ever."

"Why not?"

"I can't set them up by myself. The track's hard to get on the trestle, and I can't ever get it to work. Dad always put the whole thing together. I never learned how."

"Get the trains down, Pip," Tom said. "You're looking at a frustrated railroad man. Let's set them up."

"They're not easy to put together. You might not be able to get them to work."

"Nothing worth doing's ever easy, Pip," the man said. "You get the train down and we'll get it to work."

"Okay," Pip said, jumping to his feet. "I'll get the train stuff. Mom, can you do the dishes without me?"

"I'll do the kitchen work alone this time," she said. "You men better get that train rolling by the time I finish, though."

"Deal," Pip said, racing down the hall.

By the time Pip had located the big train box, Tom was standing at the foot of the ladder waiting.

"The box is pretty heavy, Tom," Pip said. "I'll hand it to you, okay?"

"Fire away," Tom said.

Pip pushed the heavy box to the edge of the ladder and slid it down where Tom waited. Then Tom took the heavy box and lifted it onto his broad shoulders. As the man carried the box to the living room, Pip scrambled down the ladder after him.

It took the two of them only twenty minutes to put the track together. Pip was surprised how easy it was for Tom to attach the track to the trestle. Before long, the power pack was attached to the track, and Pip was coupling the cars to the engine. When the caboose was finally hooked on, Pip sat back and waited for Tom to move the throttle. Pip could feel the power throbbing through the track.

"Go ahead," Pip told Tom. "Start it."

"Me?" Tom said. "It's your train. The throttle's all yours."

Pip's face flashed a huge smile, and the boy sprawled out on the floor and took the throttle between two of his fingers. Then Pip moved the throttle forward, and the train roared to life.

"Take it easy on the trestle," Tom warned him. "Then let the throttle go on the straightaway."

"Okay," Pip said, feeling the tension vibrating through his arms.

"Wait for me," Pip's mother called, rushing in at the last moment.

Pip eased the throttle into high gear, and the train

began roaring around the track. He gave the train steam in the straightaway, then let up on the throttle as it rounded the curves. There was a feeling of great power in Pip's hands, and a thrill raced through the boy's heart.

"It's really working!" Pip shouted as the train raced around a curve. "I only wish we had a tunnel or some mountains for it."

"It looks fine to me," his mother said. "Can I take a turn at the throttle?"

"Another frustrated engineer?" Tom asked, laughing.

Pip slowed the train and moved over to let his mother take the controls. She took the throttle, and Pip leaned against her shoulder.

"Take it easy on the throttle, Mom," Pip said.

"Thanks, little man," she said, reaching around him with her right arm and holding him tight against her shoulder.

Pip smiled as the train rolled around the track, picking up speed.

"Watch the turn!" Pip cried out.

But it was too late. The train plowed over the edge of the trestle and crashed to the floor, flinging cars in every direction.

"Some engineer!" Pip said, shutting off the power. "A wreck on your third lap!"

"Too many distractions," she said, hugging him. "It was fun, though, wasn't it?"

"Yeah," Pip said.

"Let's patch the track, Pip," Tom suggested, helping Pip remove the train from the scene of the accident.

When they had repaired the trestle and recoupled the

cars, Pip turned the controls over to Tom. The man got the train into motion, then pushed the throttle into high gear. Pip watched with his mouth open as Tom put the train into high speed. It zipped around the track. The man seemed born to have a throttle in his hand, and it was exciting to watch the train fly along.

"How do you hold it so steady?" Pip asked.

"Come over and let me show you."

Pip scooted over and watched Tom's hand on the throttle.

"It's all feeling," Tom told him. "Once you get your speed up, you have to use the curves to roll into the straightaway. You down throttle as you come into the turn. Then when you feel the train strain, you give the throttle a free hand, and the train zooms into the straightaway. You have to work at it, but once you get the feel, it's a great thrill to run the train."

"Can I try again?" Pip asked.

"It's your train. Let me put you in the groove."

Pip put his hand on the throttle. Tom placed his big hand over Pip's hand and showed him how to feel the power changes. Pip felt the shift of gravity the train encountered, and the boy soon controlled the speed of the train as nimbly as Tom did.

"You're a fast learner," Tom said, leaving Pip to run the train by himself.

"Thanks for showing me," Pip said.

The two of them sat together and ran the train for almost an hour. Then Pip's mother announced it was time for bed, and Pip switched off the train and stood up.

"Thanks for setting it up," Pip said. "I'm really too old for running trains, but it was fun."

"I don't think people are ever too old to have fun," Tom said, putting his hand on Pip's shoulder. "Games and toys are made for kids, but that doesn't mean they aren't fun for old folks, too."

"But a guy has to quit playing with trains when he gets to be twelve," Pip said.

"Why?"

"A guy has to be tough, He can't trust too many people. He has to learn how to get by, not how to play games."

"At twelve?"

"Twelve isn't so young. If I was taller, it wouldn't seem so strange. I have to help Mom more around the house. I have to start finding a job so I can pay my own way. That's the way the world works now."

"It doesn't have to be that way," Tom said. "You ought to reach out to people more, let them help."

"They try," Pip said, frowning. "But they never really help. A guy has to help himself."

"Well, we'll have to talk more about it later. Ready to hit the sack?"

"I guess so," Pip said.

Then the two of them walked into Pip's room. As Tom undressed, Pip got his clothes from a drawer and started to leave.

"Pip, hold on just a minute," Tom said.

"You need something?"

"I just wanted to ask about some of the things in your room. Are these paintings your own?"

"Everything here is mine," Pip said, glancing around the room. "It's my room."

"What I meant to ask was whether or not you'd painted them," Tom explained.

"Oh," Pip said. "I'm afraid so. They aren't too good."

"I'm the artist here. I think they're very good. When did you paint them?"

"Last fall. They have a painting class down at the Y.M.C.A. I painted things I like."

Pip sat at the foot of the bed and looked at the paintings. The first one was of a bowl of oranges. The second showed a rocket blasting off from a launching pad. The third was a mountain overlooking a lake.

"You're my kind of painter, Pip," Tom said. "You paint the things you like. That's what art is all about."

"It is?"

"Of course. A true artist portrays the things he knows and understands."

Next Tom looked over at Pip's bookshelf.

"You like science fiction, don't you?" Tom said.

"Yeah," Pip said, smiling. "I like to read. It's neat to read about other places and other times. Those science fiction books are my favorites. I dream a lot about flying off to some other planet. I think it'd be neat to see some people who are different from us. Like a Martian who's only three feet tall and has four heads."

"Who sent you the cannons?" Tom asked, pointing to the three brass cannons on Pip's dresser.

"Dad gave them to me," Pip said, frowning. "He had some toy soldiers when he was little, but he never had any cannons. He was supposed to send the soldiers, but he never did."

"What kind of soldiers?"

"You remember," Pip said. "They were supposed to

be red with black pants and white straps across their chests."

"I do remember," Tom said. "I don't suppose you'd settle for the American ones?"

"It doesn't matter now. I used to stay up all night Christmas Eve waiting for morning to come so I could open a box with soldiers in it. I always used to have a box under the tree from Dad. Then I found out Mom was buying the presents. Since then, there hasn't been anything from him."

"It's hard being forgotten, Pip."

"Well, you can't blame him. He went and got married again. He's got other kids to worry about now. I don't even get letters anymore. I guess sometimes when you get old, you forget promises."

"So that's what your mother was talking about when she told me about you and promises. You'd never break a promise, would you, Pip?"

"No way! It's not right to break a promise. Somebody might be counting on you. If you can't depend on a guy, he's nothing."

Pip stood up and walked to the door.

"I'll see you in the morning," Pip said.

"Good night, Pip."

Pip went into the living room and made his bed on the sofa. Then he slipped under the blankets and rested his head on a pillow.

In the midst of the darkness all around him, the lights on the Christmas tree twinkled on and off. It was a little bit of brightness, a little bit of life in a sea of darkness. Pip yawned, then closed his eyes.

8

Pip didn't wake up early that next morning. It was close to nine o'clock when his mother sat down on the sofa and shook his shoulder.

"Get up, Pip," she told him. "We have to get ready for church."

"It's too early," Pip complained. "Let me sleep awhile."

"Right now, young man," his mother said, pulling the blankets away so that the cold air crept through his skin.

"I surrender," Pip said, sitting up.

"Then take your shower. Tom will need to use the bathroom, too. Hurry," she said, walking away.

Pip shivered, then picked up his clothes and dashed down the hall to the bathroom, pausing only long enough to pick up a pair of pants and a clean shirt from the hall closet. Then he closed the bathroom door, locked it, and turned the water in the shower.

The shower splashed its liquid jets off his face and chest, bringing new life to his sleepy eyes. He quickly spread soap over his body and rinsed it off. Then he shampooed his hair and plunged under the water for a final rinse.

When he felt clean and refreshed, Pip turned off the water and stepped out of the shower. He dried off in a flash and started dressing. He wrapped his hair in a towel and carefully slipped his good pants on. Then he put on his shirt and his shoes and socks, carefully tying the shoelaces so that they were perfectly matched.

Then he heard a knock on the bathroom door.

"Pip, are you through yet?" Tom's voice asked through the door.

"Just about," Pip said. "You want to come in?"

"Okay," Tom said.

Pip unlocked the door and stepped aside as Tom walked in.

"You look nice this morning," Tom told him. "Your hair is a little wet, though."

"I just have to dry it. I'll move over out of your way."

Pip slid over to the edge of the dressing table and turned on the blow dryer. As the hot air fluffed his blond hair, he watched Tom take out a razor and moisten his beard. Then the man spread shaving cream over his face, covering his chin and neck. Only the lip that had the moustache was clear.

"That looks like a lot of work," Pip said.

"A man gets used to shaving, Pip," Tom told him.

"Do you have to do it every morning?"

"Every morning."

"John Mulligan has to shave about once a month. He's got a lot darker hair than me, though. I don't suppose I'll need to shave for a long time."

"Well, let's see," Tom said, pulling Pip over to the mirror. "You've got a little bit of a moustache."

"Can I shave it?"

"You don't really need to. Most boys don't shave until the hair gets in the way. Some men, like me, let their moustaches grow."

"You think I'm too young, huh?"

"Not at all, Pip. A guy's first shave ought to be helped along by a man. You get your hair dry and I'll show you how."

"Deal," Pip said, smiling broadly.

When Pip had dried his hair, he walked over and watched Tom shave. It seemed like a lot of work; Tom was very slow and careful.

"You take a lot of time, don't you?" Pip asked.

"You cut yourself a few times, it slows you down. You ready?"

"I guess."

Tom took Pip's thin shoulders in his big rough hands and held him still. Then he took a touch of shaving cream and dotted Pip's lip with it.

"Now the secret to this, Pip, is making a single clean stroke with the razor. Hold the razor firmly, but don't press it or shake it. A blade's made for cutting hair, not a man's throat or lip."

"Give me your hand."

Tom guided Pip's hand as it cut the fine little blond hairs from his lip. When they were finished, Pip looked up at the man and smiled.

"Thanks," Pip said.

"Thank you, Pip," Tom said, giving the boy's arm a

squeeze. "It's nice to share something special with a young man."

"It *was* something special," Pip said, looking into the man's eyes. "I suppose I'll remember it for a long time."

Pip brushed his hair. When he finished, the boy picked up the blue tie that he'd brought in.

"Do you suppose you could help me with this?" Pip asked.

"With what?" Tom asked, rinsing the remains of the shaving cream from his face. "A tie?"

"I can't tie it by myself," Pip said. "Mom usually does it."

"Well, it's a man's job. Let's take a crack at it."

Pip watched the man turn the piece of blue nylon into a perfect knot. Then before Pip's unbelieving eyes, the man tore the knot apart.

"Why'd you do that?" Pip asked.

"Thought the idea was for you to learn how," Tom said. "I might not be around next time."

"Okay," Pip said.

The man led Pip's fingers through the tying process. When they finished, Tom undid the knot again and gave the two ends of the tie to Pip.

"Your turn," the man said.

Pip twisted the tie around its other end until a knot was formed. Then the boy shaped it the way Tom had shown him. When he was finished, the knot was perfect.

"I did it myself," Pip said proudly.

"You sure did."

Pip turned and gave the man a huge smile. Then he

put his dirty clothes in the hamper and raced down the hall.

After a quick breakfast, the three of them headed to church. Pip rode in the back seat, humming Christmas carols as he watched Tom's eyes study his mother. When they arrived, Pip waved good-bye, then hurried off to the fellowship hall to join the youth choir. He glanced back only once to gaze at Tom leading his mother toward the sanctuary.

The Sunday before Christmas was always devoted to singing carols, and Pip sang them especially well. As he sang, he watched his mother's eyes grow brighter as she shared a hymnbook with Tom. It was impossible not to notice the love they shared. It was something truly wonderful to see, but it left Pip troubled.

One part of him wanted to rush out and hug them both, wish them the best that could be. But another part of him flashed a warning. Even the best men sometimes change. He remembered all the fathers that John Mulligan had told him about. At first John always thought they'd be real fathers. But it always turned out that they were husbands for his mother or fathers to stepbrothers and stepsisters.

It was that part of Pip that kept him from smiling, from hugging them, from telling them how happy he felt. It was that part of Pip that won out over the hoping, caring part that he wanted to trust, wanted to believe in.

Even when they got home from church, Pip didn't let himself smile. His mother and Tom spent the afternoon together in the sewing room. They kept the door closed, and Pip kept busy watching a football game with John.

"How're things going with the new guy?" John asked.

"He's not too bad," Pip said. "He showed me how to run my trains. He taught me how to tie a tie, and he helped me shave."

"You shaved?"

"Look," Pip said, pointing to his naked lip.

"You did. All the little hairs are gone."

"Told you."

"I guess you two are getting pretty close."

"I don't know. Part of me wants to be his friend. Part of me wants him for a dad. But I don't know. I'm all confused. I know better than to trust people. They make promises, then they go and break them. They're all just like my dad."

"I don't know," John said. "I never did see a man throw a football like he does."

"My dad did a lot of neat things. He made a lot of promises. But he walked out on Mom, and he left me all alone. He never even sent me the soldiers he promised."

"You don't still want them, do you?"

"I don't really need them. But I'd sure like it if my dad would send something, anything."

"I know. It's hard knowing he doesn't think about you at all."

"Well, I'm almost thirteen. It shouldn't bother me. Mom baked some cookies. You want some?"

"Sure," John said, following Pip into the kitchen.

At dinner that night everyone was strangely quiet. Pip wanted to say something, but it was easier to keep quiet. He wanted to thank Tom for all the things he'd showed him. He wanted to hug his mother and tell her he understood. But he just couldn't get the words out of his mouth.

After dinner, Pip cleared the dishes while Tom and his mother walked to the back of the house. When Pip had finished, they walked back in with sneaky smiles on their faces.

"Pip," his mother said. "Tom has something he wants to show you."

Pip followed Tom back to the sewing room. When they walked inside, he saw what Tom had been doing all day. On a small easel was a picture of a proud young wooden soldier. The soldier was dressed in a red shirt with big brass buttons. Two white straps crossed the soldier's chest, and he wore black trousers.

"It's just like the soldiers Dad promised to send," Pip said, staring at the portrait. "But the face is too friendly."

"The soldier looks like you, Pip," his mother said.

"It's really good," Pip said. He tried to force a smile onto his face, but it turned into a frown.

"But there's something wrong," Tom said, placing a big hand on Pip's shoulder. "You can tell me."

"The painting's okay, Tom," Pip said. "But you can't play with a picture. Thanks for painting it. You're a good painter."

"It was my pleasure," Tom said.

Pip looked into the eyes of the man and saw the sadness, the disappointment. It bit deep into Pip's heart to know that Tom's unhappiness was all on account of him. But Pip didn't say anything else. He ran out of the room and sat down beside the Christmas tree.

"I'm going to have a long talk with that young man," Pip heard his mother say.

"Don't," Tom's voice said. "He's trying to cope the best he knows how. I told you he wasn't ready to open up to anyone. You just have to give him time."

"And what about us?" she asked.

"Are we as important?" Tom asked. "Aren't we the ones who are grown up? Aren't we supposed to make things easier for children? It doesn't work that way very often, does it?"

"But he'd be so much better off."

"Not if he's not ready to open up. I thought he was almost there this morning. It's little enough to ask us to be patient."

"I suppose," his mother said sadly.

Pip's heart filled with sadness as he listened. He understood so much of what they felt, but he just couldn't forget all the hurting he'd done those last seven years. He couldn't forget all the afternoons he'd stood beside the mailbox and waited for the soldiers to come. It just wasn't in him to forget that much.

That night Pip slept restlessly, a great weight filling his small chest. He was confused and burdened with guilt. It was all he could do to find any sleep at all.

9

Pip slept until almost noon on Christmas Eve. It had been a sleepless night, and when his mother finally stirred him, Pip's eyes were red and full of fatigue.

"It's noon, young man," his mother said. "I'm going Christmas shopping at the mall in thirty minutes. Why don't you get up and dress? Do you have anything left to buy?"

"Oh, no," Pip said, sitting up. "I do, Mom. Let me get my clothes on and I'll go with you. Is Tom coming?"

"He's already gone," she said. "He called a cab and took off early. He said it had something to do with you."

"That figures," Pip said, frowning. "I haven't been too nice lately."

"I don't think it was anything like that," she said. "It's very mysterious."

"Well, we need a little mystery around here," Pip said, shaking himself awake. "I'll see you in a few minutes."

"You're on," she said.

Pip raced to his room and gathered some clean clothes. Then he dashed to the bathroom. After dipping in and out of a quick shower, Pip dried his hair.

As he dressed, Pip examined his lip to see if any of the hairs had started growing back. None of them had. Then he brushed his hair and met his mother in the kitchen.

"If it's okay with you Pip, we'll have lunch at the mall," she said.

"Fine with me," he told her. "Pizza?"

"All right," his mother agreed.

After they stopped in at the pizza parlor for a pepperoni pizza with anchovies, Pip and his mother went on their separate shopping missions. They agreed to meet at the supermarket at three o'clock.

Pip moved through the crowd of shoppers with ease, stepping to the side whenever someone bigger got in his way. He'd told his mother that he had several people to shop for, but he really only needed a present for Tom.

At first Pip hadn't wanted to get the man anything. He figured being nice was enough of a sacrifice to make. But that had changed. The man had done some nice things. He'd bought the big Christmas tree, set up the train set, taught Pip how to tie a tie, even helped him shave for the first time. Pip figured if Tom walked out the door and never came back, something would still last between them.

"I like him a little bit," Pip admitted to himself. "I think he likes me at least that much. He went to a lot of trouble to paint the picture, and he's tried to understand. I should at least give him a present for Christmas."

Pip walked inside the first big department store he saw. He found his way to the men's department and waited for someone to help him. He knew very little about shopping for men, but he thought about Tom and all they'd talked about. It seemed to Pip the perfect thing would be a tie.

Maybe nobody else would think of a tie as being something special, but Tom would know and understand. That was what a gift was for, anyway. Pip stepped to the counter, but the saleswoman ignored him. She hurried off to help a woman with her hands full of gifts.

It was part of being small, Pip supposed. Big people sometimes looked right over small heads. But he needed help, and he couldn't just walk away like his mother always did when she didn't get waited on.

"Can I help you?" a young woman in her twenties finally asked him.

"Yes, ma'am," Pip said. "I need to buy a tie. Can I get a nice one for seven dollars?"

"Certainly," the woman said. "Come with me. You can get a very nice tie for five dollars. We have several on sale at that price. Why don't we just take a look."

Pip followed the woman around to the tie counter. He looked at the huge assortment of ties.

"What color would you like to look at?" she asked.

"I like blue," he said. "Let's see some blue ties."

"That's my favorite color, too," she said. "How about one of these?"

"That one's nice," Pip said, pulling out a light blue tie with a yellow stripe.

"That is a nice tie. But how about this one?" she asked, showing him a darker blue tie with three thin white stripes. "I bought one like this for my boyfriend. It's really nice."

"It's pretty. Would a man about thirty-five go for it?"

"I would think so."

"Okay, I'll take it."

"Come on, then. Let's ring it up."

"Could you gift wrap it, too? I don't want my mother to know about it."

"A secret from Mom and Dad, huh?" she asked.

"I haven't got a dad. It's for a friend of hers."

"Well, who knows?" she said, smiling at him. "Maybe next year it will be Dad."

Pip just stared at the ceiling. The woman wrapped the tie and put a pretty bow on it. Then he paid her and walked out of the store.

When he met his mother at three, she had her arms filled with packages. They set them all down in the back seat, then went inside the grocery store to do the shopping.

Pip picked out the Christmas candy and the eggnog. He also remembered to buy a card for the tie. Then they ran the groceries through the check stand and made their way to the car. When they got home, Pip helped his mother unload the groceries. Then he dashed into the living room and opened the card.

"Thanks for the stories, the trains, the tie, and the picture," Pip wrote.

He signed the card with his whole name, Phillip E. North. Then he placed the card in its envelope, taped the envelope to the box and wrote "To Tom" on the outside. As Pip was putting the box under the Christmas tree, his mother walked in and sat down beside him.

"Thank you, Pip," she said, kissing him on the cheek. "You'll never know how much this will mean to Tom. He's been worried that you don't like him."

"It's just a thank you," he told her. "Nothing more."

She looked into his solemn eyes and frowned.

"He really likes you, Pip. You have a way of reaching people. I don't know what it is. I don't have it. Try as I may, I can't ever get people to fall all over themselves to get to know me. But there's something in those eyes of yours that reaches right into the heart of a person."

"He's been nice. But I can't care about anybody besides you. It's too risky."

"Your father really hurt you, Pip," she said, hugging him close to her. "If ever there's justice in this life, I hope someone hurts him as bad sometime."

"No, Mom. I hope no one ever hurts as bad as I used to."

"Used to?" she asked.

"Well, I'm old enough to take things now. Used to be, I'd get all upset about things. Like crying because he never wrote to me at Christmas. But it wasn't because I did something wrong. Now I just blow it off."

"I wish you'd give Tom a chance. I really thought yesterday morning that you two were on the road to being great friends."

Pip turned away from her and sat back on the sofa.

"What's wrong?" she asked.

"Nothing," he mumbled.

"Tell me, Pip. This is your mother, not some police interrogator."

"If you marry him, you won't have any time for me. I'll be just like John Mulligan."

"No, Pip. You'd have two parents instead of one."

"It starts out that way, but it always ends the same. I'd be left out."

His mother looked at him with hurt eyes. She brushed a tear away from her eye and walked out of the living room. Pip could hear her crying in the kitchen.

At dinner there was a wall of silence between them all. The roast beef was eaten. The mashed potatoes disappeared. The carrots and peas and pie were gobbled up, but no one said a single word.

That night as Pip lay on the sofa with his eyes closed, he heard them walk by and stop, whispering.

"Look how peaceful he sleeps," his mother said. "You'd never know there were a thousand worries wound up in that little head of his."

"I wish I could lift all those worries from him and put them on my shoulders," Tom said. "I wish I'd been his father. I promise you I wouldn't have let him down."

"You don't let down anyone but yourself," Pip's mother said. "You worry about others so much you don't enjoy life. Like taking care of your brother's business for five years. You can't live your life for other people all the time."

"I haven't," he said. "I had my fling. I spent five years in Europe, painting and drawing. But those years were like a dream, and I had to wake up sometime. Now I've got a good job, a fine future. If I could only sketch you and Pip into it."

"You can," she said.

"You know that would be wrong with him feeling the way he does. You know I spent all day driving from shopping center to shopping center trying to find those toy soldiers. It doesn't make any sense to him, but he wants them more than a trip to the moon."

"His father promised to send them. Pip has this thing about promises. He feels he can't trust anyone because his father let him down."

"You can't blame him. He thinks I've come here to take you away from him. He doesn't understand I want him, too. He can't understand that I love you, and since he's a part of you, I love him, too."

"I don't think it's that."

"It's exactly that. If I just could have found those soldiers. They just don't make them anymore."

"Tom, that was his father's promise. Sooner or later he has to know you're not going to be his father."

"I want to be his father. Besides, a boy should have promises made to him kept. If I'm going to make this work between us, I have to prove to him I can make up for the hurt and disappointment his father brought him."

"I'm not sure that's possible."

"It better be."

"What will we tell him about our plans?"

"Nothing," Tom answered. "I had hoped he'd learn to trust me, to love me a little, at least to accept me. I care for him, I really do. You know that. But if I came in here and disturbed his world, upset the little security he still has, I just don't think he'd forgive me. I won't bring more pain to that boy. I just won't do that."

"He likes you."

"In time maybe he will. Right now I'm a threat to

him. Oh, I wish I had those soldiers. I wish I had some small way of cutting the ice, of breaking through that wall he's built around his feelings. I want to go over there right now and take him in my arms and hug him. I want to tell him that everything will be all right and that he can trust me."

"Why don't you?"

"It would never work. He's not seven years old. He's very grown up, even if he doesn't look it. I wouldn't want him any other way. This thing has to be on his terms. If we wait long enough, I think the three of us can be a real family. I don't think either of us wants a family that would exclude Pip."

"No," she sighed. "But I need you so much, Tom."

"I need you, too, Ellen, but we have a lot of years left. For Pip, every single day is a lifetime."

"But you'd be good for him."

"Only if he wanted me."

Pip cried inside as he listened to them walk away. He knew he was hurting them both, but he just couldn't break down that wall he'd built. Seven years of mistrust couldn't be patched up with a few days of stories and promises.

10

Pip woke up Christmas morning when his mother put her soft hand on his shoulder. He came to life slowly, looking up at her with his big blue eyes.

"Merry Christmas," he said, hugging her.

"Merry Christmas, honey," she said.

"It's awful quiet," Pip said. "Where's Tom?"

"He's been acting very strangely. We got up early and had breakfast. Then he got a phone call and took the car. He said he had to meet a train."

"That's weird," Pip said, sitting up. "I guess I'd better get dressed. He's coming back, isn't he?"

"I hope so. He's got the car."

"He's not the kind that would run out without telling you," Pip said. "He's a pretty okay guy, I guess."

"Get dressed and come into the kitchen. I'd like to talk with you about him."

"Okay," Pip said, walking into the bathroom to get his clothes on.

When he was dressed, Pip walked into the kitchen and sat down at the table. His mother brought him a plate of ham and eggs, and he started eating slowly. She sat down next to him and looked at him seriously.

"I want to talk to you about Tom," she said.

"Okay," Pip said, trying to avoid her eyes.

"He's a very rare man, Pip. I've never known anyone quite like him. He gave up five years of his life to go home to Vermont and straighten out his brother's advertising business. He's been nearly everywhere. He's one of the top five commercial artists in the country. He could make a quarter million dollars a year in New York, but he's willing to take a fifth of that to come to Texas and be near us.

"Pip, since your father left us, Tom's the first man I've felt anything for. I know what it's like to mistrust people. I was suspicious of every word, every glance a man gave me. But Pip, you can't spend your whole life afraid of people. You can't live alone. You need people. And Tom is the best. If you'd give him a chance, he could make life so much easier for you. And for me."

"I know all that, Mom. I want you to be happy. You're not too old to have kids, and if I weren't around, you'd have gotten married by now."

"But you are here, Pip, and I wouldn't trade you for the rest of the world. You know that. I don't want Tom just for myself. I want him for you, too. You should have a man you can depend on."

"I don't need anything."

"You do, too. You need someone to teach you all the things I can't. You need a man for that. I can't explain all the new feelings you're going to have. I can't laugh with you about hairy chests. Pip, you're the best. All I want is the best for you."

"I know, Mom. But I just can't change how I feel. I love you, and I want the best for you, too. I just can't be sure. Mom, this guy makes a lot of promises. Promises get broken. I can't stand the idea of another guy leaving us."

"You read people very well, Pip. You know Tom would never turn his back on you or me. He's been here only five days, but you've already made a place for yourself in his heart. Hasn't he made even a small dent in you?"

"Sure he has, Mom. But a guy can't trust his heart. He has to remember."

"I'm sorry you feel that way, Pip," she said sadly. "If ever three people belonged together, we three do."

"Mom, I wish sometimes I could do what you ask. I wish I could have a new father who would love me and talk to me, and do things with me. But, Mom, it doesn't work that way. My friends have new fathers, a lot of them. It's always the same. They start out trusting the guys and end up getting hurt."

"It's not always that way," his mother said with tears in her eyes.

Pip sat back, his eyes mirroring her sadness. Then he finished his breakfast. As he was eating the last bite, he heard the car pull into the driveway. His mother sat up, then walked over to the door that led to the garage. She walked back alone, though.

"Wasn't that Tom?" Pip asked.

"I thought so," she said.

Then the front door opened, and Pip's mother raced into the living room. Pip just sat back and sighed. He was in no hurry to continue their conversation. He didn't want Christmas morning spoiled by an argument.

Then Tom and his mother walked into the kitchen with bright smiles.

"Merry Christmas," Tom said, grabbing Pip's arm. "Let's go see what we got for Christmas."

There was something magical about Tom's smile, and Pip followed him like a rat following the Pied Piper. When they reached the living room, Pip froze. There, spread out in marching formation, were twenty-four wooden soldiers. They wore the blue uniforms of Continental grenadiers.

"You're too old to believe in Santa Claus, Pip, so I'll admit they're from me," Tom told him. "I hope it doesn't ruin things for them to be blue."

"But how?" Pip asked.

"Well, I found out how much you wanted the soldiers, so on Saturday morning I went to a phone booth to call my family in Vermont and ask them to send my soldiers right away. Meanwhile, I looked around town in case mine didn't arrive on time. The train depot called this morning so I went to pick them up. My father was a carpenter, and he made these for me when I was a little younger than you."

"That's a whole lot of trouble," Pip said. "All that just because I wanted some toy soldiers."

"All that because you were promised them," Tom said. "Promises are important. When a boy's twelve, he ought to have promises kept to him. When something's important to you, then you should have it."

Pip sat down on the floor and looked at the soldiers.

Each one was painted by hand. They were like nothing he'd ever seen.

"The one with the epaulets on his shoulders is supposed to be Ethan Allen," Tom said, sitting down beside Pip.

Pip just sat there. It was all Pip could do to keep from crying. Tom's strong arms reached around the boy and hugged him close. Pip felt the warmth flow from Tom, and the wall Pip had kept up so long toppled. Pip wrapped his small arms around Tom and hugged him tightly.

"You know, Pip," Tom said, choking back some tears, "your mom and I've been thinking about getting hitched. What would you think about that?"

"I think you'd better do it," Pip said, trying to keep back a laugh. "I'm getting tired of sleeping on the sofa."

"Why you," his mother said, tickling him. "You think we're going to let you get away with that?"

"Sure," Pip said. "You'll let me say anything as long as I'll go along with things."

"Is that what you're doing?" Tom asked. "Going along with things?"

"No," Pip said. "I like it just fine."

"You really wouldn't mind us getting married?" his mother asked.

"That depends," Pip said. "Could I start calling Tom Dad?"

"You'd better," Tom said, hugging him a second time.

After they had opened their presents, Pip felt himself warm all over. Tom had put the blue tie on, and somehow they had become a family.

When the torn paper and discarded bows were put

away, Pip sat down on the piano bench and played Christmas carols. On his right side, his mother sang softly in her high, clear voice. On his left side, Tom joined in with his deep, firm baritone.

As they sang, Pip felt wonderful. He sat in the middle of their love, but he wasn't in the way. He found comfort in Tom's shoulders in the same way he felt it in his mother's softness.

Pip knew there would be problems ahead, just as there were in any family. But he also knew he'd always be able to trust Tom's promises, and he'd find ears willing to listen to whatever he had to say.

As they sang "Silent Night," the three of them hugged each other tightly, and they knew there would never again be a wall between any of them.